MW01223313

The FISHER of BONES

by Sarah Gailey

Fireside
BOOKS

Edited by Brian J. White
Cover illustration by Miranda Meeks
Book design by Pablo Defendini

Published by Fireside Fiction Company
Brooklyn, NYC

firesidefiction.com
ISBN: 978-0-9987783-2-7

Content Notes

Fireside Fiction Company provides content notes for its books to guide readers who may wish to seek out or avoid particular story elements. These content notes may contain spoilers. The content note for *The Fisher of Bones* is at the end of this book, on page 97.

A current list of all the elements covered in our content notes can be found on our website: *firesidefiction.com/about/#content-notes*.

The FISHER of BONES

Contents

CHAPTER ONE

ḷaming

THE MOON WAS DARK the night our Prophet died.

Outside of his tent, Margot the healer wept, her hands clutching at the white stubble on her scalp. Black vines of withdrawn illness clung to her wrists, thick and steaming and insoluble. She hadn't taken breaks to shave — nor to eat, nor to s leep — over the six days and nights she'd spent trying to hold back the strangling blisters that crept up the Prophet's chest. It was obvious that she'd done all she could. We couldn't hold this death against her. The illness was stronger than Margot's magic. It was stronger than anyone's magic.

It was an ordained death, and nothing less.

The Prophet said as much. He told me in his final hour, just before he banished me.

———

When the Prophet was a young man, he fled the hundred eyes of his city, and he found himself lost in a field. It was there that he discovered the bone tablets, which were half-buried in mud so thick he lost his shoes in it. He tripped over the tablets in his bare feet, and when he pried the strange slabs from the mud, he saw them to be bone, and he saw them to be etched with letters that no man could read. And when he looked upon the writing, his eyes were opened by the Gods, and he no longer feared the beating that awaited him at the Chancellor's House, for he saw his purpose.

———

He was looking at me with eyes that were dark like the death-moon, black from edge to edge, stained by Gods Sight. They'd frightened me when I was a child, before I learned to look for the creases at the corners. "Take care of Margot," he said.

"I'll take care of all of them," I said, and my voice didn't tremble even though it should have. He snorted at me.

"You know what I mean. Be kind to her in the next few days," he said. "She's sensitive. She'll blame herself. Counsel her to—"

"Trust in the Gods. I know," I said. There I went, getting impatient with a man whose cheek was turned toward the sunlight of his own death. I studied his weather-beaten face, suddenly desperate. "Surely there's more I need to know. Surely there's more you have to tell me, I'm not ready for—"

He patted my wrist weakly, the sun-bruised brown of his hand two shades darker than mine, tanned from always pointing the way. He cleared his throat. "Ducky," he said, and the first tears blurred my vision. "Listen. I know I haven't always been the best father."

Oh.

That.

———

It was the Gods' own magic that worked through the young man who would become the Prophet. Everyone knew that the Gods had been cast out when the Chancellor came to power. Everyone knew that the Gods were illegal — the only thing worth worshipping in the Chancellor's city was work. Everyone knew that. But none of them knew that the Gods were waiting for their children to follow them out of the City.

No one except the Prophet.

And when the young man touched the tablets, the Gods' own magic opened his eyes, and he gathered his people to him, the children of the Gods. And they set out into the wastelands outside the city, and they began the journey.

———

"I'm sorry, Ducky. I know that leading these people has kept me from you. I wasn't there for you after your mother died, and that— it wasn't right. You shouldn't have been alone then." He stared at me with those dark eyes. "And I know I've been hard on you these past few years, trying to get you ready. But I hope you know how much I love you. How much I've always loved you."

"I know, Dad," I whispered, and my voice did tremble that time, because there was a lie there. I was never a good liar.

And then his breath rattled in his chest, and it was soon, and we both knew it. He laid a hand on my forehead, and his hand was cold, and I wasn't ready.

"I hereby—" he paused for breath, and when he spoke again, his voice rang out louder than it's possible for a man to speak. Loud enough for the two hundred ears in the camp to hear. I wanted to say *don't* — wanted to tell him not to use the last of his strength for this, wanted to tell him to give me just thirty minutes more, I had so many questions, please, no, *I'm not ready* — but one mustn't interrupt a Prophet when he's Speaking.

So I closed my eyes and listened.

———

The Gods' instructions, legible only to the Prophet, spoke of the journey. Come, they said, and arrive at the appointed hour, and we shall be awaiting you with open arms. The land is a land of plenty. Rich hunting and plentiful fish and good, clear waters await you, and your spawn shall be many, and no harm shall befall you from above or below. Come at the appointed hour, do not be late, and we shall welcome you.

And the Prophet and his people followed the directions on the tablet, and walked by moonlight, and for thirty years, they came ever closer to the Land of Plenty.

And the Prophet Spoke.

"I hereby deny you, Ducky, daughter of Fisher. You are banished. Be forever cast out from your people, a stranger to them from this day until the day of your death. Never return to this place."

A chill washed over me. This was the Gods' own magic, working through the Prophet, banishing me from my home and into the wastelands that surrounded our camp. He paused for breath again. He coughed, seemed to deflate around the sickness that had crept into his lungs. *No, please* — but then he licked his lips and the hand on my forehead warmed with the last of his life, and this was it, and I wasn't ready, but that didn't matter.

It was time.

"Greetings, foundling. I hereby name you in the sight of the Gods and their people: Fisher, Prophetess, leader of the children of the Gods. By this name you shall be known to your people; by this name they shall follow you. Go forth, Prophetess, and lead your people to the Land of Plenty."

As his voice faded, a wail rose from the people of the camp. Unfamiliar, unnatural warmth stole through me, and a shimmer crossed my vision, and I knew that the next child to see my eyes would know the fear I'd felt when I was a girl. The Gods' own magic, passing from him to me.

He whispered one more thing, in a voice that was only for my ears. "You will lead them well," he said, and I shivered like a wet lamb.

My father died with one palm resting on the tablets, and the other still resting on my forehead. As his breath left him, my new name settled over me.

Leader of the children of the Gods. Fisher. Prophetess.

Orphan.

CHAPTER TWO

Cycle

THE GODS WHISPERS woke me in the night. My eyes opened and at first I grabbed for Marc, but I stopped myself before my hand could land on my sleeping husband's bare chest. My palm hovered over his heart, just above the thick carpet of blonde hair that stretched between his nipples and his navel.

When they come, I remembered my father the Prophet saying, *you'll know to listen.*

So I rose from our sleeping mat and stood with my palms open. And I listened.

The Gods Whispers were unintelligible, shushing and sloshing and occasionally making me feel unsteady on my feet. I closed my eyes and practiced breathing the way the Prophet had taught me to, as though the air was thick and heavy, and I caught a single word out of the strange rush of sound.

Go.

So I went.

———

I stood outside beneath the light of a sharp crescent moon. The desert sand retained a little of the day's warmth, but the night air still bit at my elbows and throat, and I pulled my cloak tighter in an attempt to transform the itch of the fabric into warmth.

Behind me, my new tent: large, with two flaps in the front and enough room to stand comfortably. It was patched and wearing thin at the folds. It was fragrant, the odor of decades of human occupation masked by the recent smells of clove and beeswax and juniper. It was the tent in which my father had died.

In front of me, my old tent: low and small and identical to the sixty other tents in the camp. The sides fluttered, and the lantern in front of the stakes was dark. Even before I peeked inside, I knew that its new occupant was not inside. Hanna, the huntress, was gone.

I let the tentflap fall, and the Gods Whispers began afresh. The light of the crescent moon fell upon a shadow near my feet.

I looked down. I was wrong: it was not a shadow.

It was blood. Rich and fragrant. The breeze that bothered Hanna's tentflap lifted the smell of it to me, and I made the sign of the moon over my head.

"Thank you, Holiest, for your gift of blood." I whispered the same blessing I'd said every month since my girlhood, a reflex at the sight and the smell of the blood. It took on a new meaning as I realized that the Gods must have gifted Hanna with an especially heavy month, to leave such clear footprints in sand. I knelt and touched my fingers to the sand next to the stain, tracing the outline of a footprint. "Where are you going, Hanna?"

———

Perhaps she just needed to relieve herself. Perhaps that's why she wandered into the desert in the middle of the night without alerting anyone to her departure. Perhaps she ate something spoiled, and she had to leave urgently, and that's why she didn't light the lantern that sits outside of every tent to indicate that the occupant is coming right back. Perhaps she was tracking some night-dwelling creature and she heard it, and she ran out of her tent without thinking to grab the bow that leaned against the side of the canvas.

I came up with many answers as I followed Hanna's red-brown footprints into the desert. The Gods Whispers hushed around me, and I knew that none of my answers were correct.

"I can't believe she's making us wait another night to break camp." The voice travelled to me from the other side of a dune, and I stopped moving. The Gods Whispers fell silent. I crouched and held my breath as the sand nudged against my feet.

"Can Fisher even read the tablets?"

"Her father said—"

"Her father is dead." Hanna. That was Hanna's voice, flat and calm and authoritative. She'd always been good at speaking fact into uncertainty. There were four other voices — no, five. I tried to identify them as they argued about whether I could be trusted with leadership. The Prophet would have been able to identify them. He would have known them by a single word, by a single *breath*.

"I think — hm. I think that we should wait and see." There, I knew that voice — that was Liam, the seed-tender. That was his funny little cough. I'd heard it dozens of times, playing in the seed-wagon as a girl. I sat back on my heels, pressing my fingers into the sand, digging for the warm layer that would be a foot beneath the surface. "Maybe she'll be useful. And if she's not—"

The Gods Whispers started up again. The same as the ones that had woken me up. *Go.*

I fled back to my tent. *Stupid*, I thought as I ran across the sand, *stupid* — if they had come over the dune, there would have been nowhere for me to hide. They would have known that I'd heard them. *And if she's not...?*

I crawled into the bed beside Marc, my feet tracking sand onto our sleeping mat, my cloak a dusty puddle of wool at the entrance to our tent. He shifted to accommodate me, his arm nudging under my head, his stubble rasping at the back of my neck.

"Everything all right?" His baritone whisper was so much clearer than that of the Gods.

"Do you think I can do this?" I whispered back. His lips brushed the nape of my neck.

"Your father thought you could do it," he said. "Where did you go?"

I let a few breaths pass before answering. "Nowhere," I finally replied. "We should break camp tomorrow," I added.

"Mm." His breath slowed, and then he was asleep behind me, his chest pressed close to my back, our legs tangled together.

Silently, so as not to wake him, I started to thank the Gods for showing me the bloody footprints in the sand. I thanked them for the fact that Hanna had chosen to rally against me at the same time that she was being visited. I was going to thank them even for her treachery — I couldn't see how it was a gift, but the Gods give only gifts, and they must be thanked for each and every one.

But something caught in my mind as I was giving thanks.

Hanna's bloody footprints in the sand. The fragrance of Hanna's blood, sacred and sharp and musky on the night air.

It was a fragrance I hadn't smelled in too long.

I thought back to the last time I'd left bloody footprints of my own. It had been on the rock-flats, after we'd passed the giant arches of stone but before the Prophet had taken ill. I counted moons in my mind: dead, crescent, quarter, gibbous, Godsmoon, waning, quarter, crescent, and then the dead moon when the healer had failed and the Prophet had died — and then again, all the way until tonight's crescent.

I counted again. It could not be. It *could not be*.

I counted a final time, and then the Gods Whispers began to rustle, and I could not deny it any longer.

I made the sign of the moon, and I thanked the Gods even as I wept for the blood that I knew would not come for seven more months. I lay awake, weeping and praying, as careful footfalls passed outside my tent. I rested a palm against my belly, and I did not wake Marc. Not yet.

"The Gods give only gifts," I reminded myself. I repeated it a hundred times over before the dawn broke over the tents of my people.

CHAPTER THREE

Increase

"You should eat more."

Marc made as if to hand me the remainder of his bread. It was all he'd have to eat that day — the tablets had predicted a shortage of food during the end of the first quarter-moon, so we were on rations. I pushed it back to him.

"I'm not hungry," I lied. Outside, the sound of mallets driving stakes through the corners of tents echoed throughout the camp. Under the constant high drone of emptiness in my stomach, a tiny heartbeat fluttered.

"Please, Fisher," he said. He hadn't called me Ducky since the night of my father's death. No one had. "I don't need it. You do. You... both do." He aimed a significant glance at my abdomen and I had a sudden urge to hit him.

"We all do," came a voice from behind me. I turned and saw Rand, the child-minder. Marc's older brother. He had a face like a dog's, soft-eyed and worried, but his mouth was eternally pinched into an I-know-better line.

The tablets say not to hate anyone, and so I did not hate Rand.

"Why are we on rations, Prophetess?" Rand asked. "There's more than enough food to go around. Why are my children hungry?"

"I told you yesterday, Rand," I said in a tone that I hoped was a model of patience and understanding. "The tablets say that there will not be enough food for everyone as we leave the desert to enter the rock barrens. The tablets recommend—"

"Can you even *read* the tablets?"

Marc took a step forward, radiating anger like a live coal. "Of course she can read the tablets, look at her eyes, any damned fool can—"

"What?" Rand challenged. "Can what? Can take all the food for herself while she leaves her people to starve? Just because your brat is in her belly—"

"Watch yourself, brother," Marc growled, and they were too close together and Rand's lip was lifting into a snarl—

But then Hanna came running, shouting my name. She skidded to a halt just a few feet from where the two men stood. "Sorry," she said breathlessly, "there's an emergen— there's a *situation*."

I nodded for her to continue, leaving Rand and Marc to either fight or cease their snarling.

"I was in the sands," Hanna said, her breathing already slowing. I took in her scarves and her long sleeves and her tight-wrapped legs, and I knew that she had almost certainly been hunting. She almost certainly hadn't snuck into the desert again to plot against me. Almost certainly. "I was getting a sense of the land — looking for spoor, tracks," she continued, "and I saw — I saw people. I found people."

I stared at her. "What?"

"I found *people*," she repeated.

I was dumbstruck. The route the tablets took us on kept us far from the high-walled cities of the North, East, and South, and we weren't crossing into any of the Western mining territories or military training facilities of the Citadel. "That can't be," I said stupidly. "There's... there's nobody *here*."

She shook her head. "I thought I was seeing things, but... come see for yourself," she said.

"You brought them back with you?!" My voice was shrill in my own ears, and I put up a hand before she could respond. "Sorry, I— this is a lot to take in. Where are they?"

She looked uncomfortable. "They're in your tent," she said in a low tone. "Sorry, Fisher. I figured you'd want to decide what to do with them before we let anyone else see them."

Without another word, we started walking to my tent. Her stride was long, longer than mine, but she shortened it so as not to make me jog after her, and I was grateful. I glanced at her sidelong and wondered if I'd been wrong to question her loyalty.

———

It took a few seconds for my vision to adjust to the darkness of my tent. I must have looked imposing to them — a strange, breathless woman bursting through the canvas and then standing silently for the space of five heartbeats. Finally, my eyes acclimated, and the vague shadows before me resolved into the shape of a person. A stout woman in a full skirt, her hair a redder brown than that of any of the travelers in my camp. Her strangely-shadowed face was so sunburnt that I flinched to look at it; a blister stood out on her nose.

"I thought you said there were two?" I muttered. Hanna nodded, gestured, and a piece of the woman's skirt broke away. I made an involuntary noise and felt my fingers brush my lips before I knew I was covering my mouth.

The woman was not stout, and her skirt was not full. There was a boy. Five, I thought, or a malnourished seven. He had her same strange, red-brown hair. He'd been hiding his face, and his dust-shrouded clothing had blended perfectly with her robes. The two of them stood side-by-side, and I realized that the strange shadows on the woman's face were the outlines of her skull.

They were starving.

"Broth," I murmured to Hanna. "Bring broth, now."

"But the rationing—"

"Now," I snapped, and she gave me a cold, close-lipped nod before leaving the tent.

I took a deep breath, then heard a sniffle behind me. I turned around to see the skeletal boy wiping his nose on his sleeve. "There's no need to cry anymore," I said, attempting a beatific smile. "You're home now, friends."

The boy lifted his eyes to mine. The moment he saw my God-stained eyes, he burst into terrified, uncomprehending tears. The woman's knees buckled, and the boy let out a wail as she collapsed.

———

"They can't stay," Marc murmured into my ear as people — my people — gathered in the center of the encampment. "There's not enough food."

"They won't eat much," I said back. "It'll take them at least a couple of weeks to re-acclimate to a normal diet, and by then we'll be in the grasslands again."

"They'll slow us down, and we're already behind," he hissed at me. "We can't afford to wait for them to be well, and we can't afford the resources." Liam, standing a few feet away, turned to see what we were whispering about. He was still holding the mallet he'd been using to stake down tents. I gave him a tight smile.

"This isn't a discussion, Marc," I said. "I'm not sending them back into the sands to die."

"I'm just saying what everyone else is going to say," he replied mulishly. "We don't even know who these people *are*. They could be criminals."

"The tablets are clear on this," I said, and turned to him with my eyes wide, so he could see the expansive blackness of the Gods Sight. "*Sanctuary shall be offered to any traveler in their hour of need, be they crawling creature or vast leviathan. Forget not the Sanctuary, lest you be turned away onto the sands.*"

He frowned at me, not looking directly into my eyes. I laid a palm over my abdomen to remind myself that I loved him. That we loved each other enough to make a child. That we loved each other enough to disagree. I offered my cheek, and he kissed it once, lightly, before taking his seat in the crowd.

I turned to face my people, and raised my hands high. "Friends," I began, "I have gathered you here today to welcome two newcomers into our midst." A murmur began in the crowd, and I cleared my throat. I kept my hands up and spoke over them. "These two—"

"What are they gonna eat?" I followed the direction of turning heads until my eyes landed on Liam. His arms were folded over his barrel chest.

"That is for the healer to decide." I did not mention that Margot had been weak and unsteady since her failure to heal the Prophet. "I anticipate that it will be little, as they have been starving since at least the last gibbous moon," I said, before continuing in the formal voice with which a Prophetess should address her people. "These two newcomers come from a city far to the North." There was murmuring as people began to speculate about the notoriously brutal cities. I cut it off with a raised hand. "They have been wandering for many days and many nights. They are injured, starving, and ill. We have offered them Sanctuary, and with eyes open to our mission, they have accepted. We are gathered tonight to name and welcome them. They are in Margot's tent tonight, but have consented to be named in absentia." Another murmur from the crowd. I ignored it.

I looked up at the rising moon, just two handspans above the horizon, and opened my throat to the Gods. *When the time comes*, my father had said, *you'll know how*.

"Greetings, foundlings," I said, my arms held out to the side as though I would embrace the low-slung moon. My voice echoed throughout the encampment, over the sands. I knew that the woman and the child could hear me. For all I knew, the city they'd fled could hear me, too. "I, Fisher, hereby name you in the sight of the Gods and their people, the names you have chosen in the sight of the Prophetess, the Healer, and all the Gods: Maia and Samuel. By these names you are welcomed. By these names you shall be known to your people; by this name they shall harbor you. Maia and Samuel, welcome home."

All around me, my people cheered. I looked into their faces, and saw the silence that rested heavily on some of their faces. More than just Liam and Rand and Hanna.

I raised my hands skyward and repeated myself for the benefit of the silent, looking at each one in turn. "Welcome home."

CHAPTER FOUR

Loss

MARGOT SHIVERED AGAIN. She wouldn't stop shivering.

I worried at my lower lip and put another blanket over her. Outside of the tent, a child shrieked, and answering footfalls spoke to a game of chase or tag or perhaps just "run run run." The sound of their game faded fast, and soon, all I could hear was Margot, the healer, breathing hard and shallow. I waited until her eyelids drifted shut before sliding my sandals on and slipping out through the tentflap.

I blinked into the grey light of the morning mist, wiping sweat from my brow. The wispy fog that clung to the camp rendered the day eerily quiet — the crunch of the gravel under my sandals seemed overloud. The running children were already well out of earshot. I passed dewdrop-covered tents, the families inside enjoying a morning's rest. The transition from the sands to the rock flats had been a taxing one, steep and arduous. Two wagons had thrown wheels, and the seed-wagon's axle had split, and we'd had to slaughter a good ox after his leg fractured under the strain of the climb. Everyone was tired, snippy. I'd already decided to take a day's rest, even before Margot had gotten sick.

"Please, please, please preserve her," I prayed under my breath. "Please."

The Gods did not answer.

"Are you talking to yourself?" A face appeared out of the mist, and I smiled even as I saw my friend's eyes flick away from mine. Naomi still wasn't used to the Gods Sight. I couldn't blame her.

"It sure feels like it sometimes," I said. "What are you doing up?"

"Checking the oxen," she said, running a hand through her short cap of tight blonde curls. They had relaxed into loose waves while we were on the sands, but the low-slung clouds on the rock flats had sprung them back into spirals, and I couldn't help thinking the humidity suited her. "If we lose another one, we'll have to abandon a wagon."

She looked at me, her mouth pinched with expectation, and I realized that she wasn't talking to me as her friend. She was talking to me as her Prophetess. "Oh," I said, blinking a few times. "Oh, right. We, uh, we would probably need to abandon the children's wagon, right?"

She gave me a gentle smile. "We abandoned that one when we came down the mountain into the sands," she said softly. I chastised myself for missing that — but then I remembered with a start that when we'd come down the mountain into the sands, my father had begun to die. "I think we'd need to consider consolidating the water wagon and the seed wagon."

I laughed, a short, sharp bark that was swallowed by the mist. "I'll let you be the one to tell Liam that," I said, and her smile twitched. I cleared my throat. "Is there anything that can be done to keep us from losing an animal? We only have to stretch them for nine more months." I tried hard to keep a note of pleading from entering my voice.

"Is that guaranteed?" she murmured, and if she hadn't been my best friend — but then I remembered that I was the Prophetess, and that I had a job to do.

"It is written," I said, gentle but stern. "It will come to pass. Nine more months."

"Right," she said. "Sorry." She still wouldn't meet my eyes.

I suppressed a sigh. "So, anything I can do to help get us there?"

"I'd like to have Margot take a look at a few of the beasts," she said.

"Margot's sick," I said. "She's — I don't think she's up for it."

"Sick?" Naomi's brow creased. "Margot can't get sick. Healers never get sick."

I shrugged. "I don't know. It's... I shouldn't go into details, but." *But it looks bad. But I don't know how to fix it. But I'm afraid.* "But I can't make her come do an exam."

Naomi waved her hand, tossing her curls. "She's probably just tired," she said. "We're all tired, Fisher. You can send her over once she's rested, yeah? I've done what I can for the animals, but it's hard to identify weaknesses in the bones and I'm worried about—"

"She can't help you," I interrupted. Her mouth snapped shut with a click of teeth. "Is there anything else?"

Her nostrils flared, and a muscle jumped in her jaw several times before she finally bit out an answer. "I suppose you could pray, *Prophetess.*"

I nodded. "I always do."

—

The mist was still low by the time I came back to Margot's tent. A bowl of broth steamed in my hand, a match to the one that warmed my belly. A few precious shreds of uncured ox haunch floated in the bowl, my own ration as well as Margot's. The majority of the animal was already packed in salt, but this, at least, we could spare.

I knelt at the edge of the healer's sleeping mat, balancing the broth in one hand. I touched the back of my hand to her forehead in a vague echo of a fuzzy childhood memory: my mother's cool fingers on my own blazing cheeks.

Except that Margot's skin wasn't blazing. She'd been shivering all night, grappling with an untenable fever, reminding me more of my father with every passing moment — but now, her forehead was cool. Her fever had broken.

"Thank the Gods," I whispered, "Thank you, thank you, thank you." Relief and fatigue made me suddenly giddy. I set the bowl down beside her and sprang up to find Naomi, to tell her that Margot would be able to check the beasts of burden the next day, once she'd finished recovering. But as I reached for the tentflap, something shifted in my belly. I pressed my palm to the shallow rise of my abdomen, and felt the shift again — the bottom dropping out of a bottle, the brush of a finger against my cheek in the night. Gods Whispers rose around me like the crashing of waves.

I turned around and looked to Margot again. My eyes slid away from her face, and I looked at the bowl of broth next to her. Steam no longer rose from the surface of the bowl. A chill passed through the room.

It was the chill of a light extinguishing.

I looked back at Margot. Slowly, I stepped back toward her. My breathing was loud inside the tent, too loud. I inhaled deeply through my nose and then did not breathe again.

The Gods Whispers ceased. The tent was silent.

"Oh," I whispered. "Oh, no." I reached for Margot's cool, clammy face. Her skin still felt like skin; her cheeks were the same shade of brown that they had been before she took ill. I pressed a finger to the underside of her jaw, to the inside of her wrist. I pressed my ear to her chest, and when I lifted my head, two broad dark tearstains marked the sheet that covered her.

I sat back on my heels and stared at the dead healer, and waited for Gods Whispers to return and guide me. I waited for them to tell me what to do, how to proceed, how to tell my people that the only healer in their midst was gone.

But the Gods Whispers did not come.

CHAPTER FIVE

fear

"PLEASE O GODS, REVEAL UNTO ME YOUR WISDOM."

I spoke the words with sincerity in my heart as I prepared to open the chest that contained the Word of the Gods. It was a prayer that I was meant to repeat before looking at the tablets, although my father had told me once that forgetting the prayer didn't prevent the Gods Sight from working.

Still.

I dipped my fingers into the divot in the top of the chest and touched them to my tongue. The Prophet — my father — had carved it, along with the rest of the chest, according to a vision sent by the Gods on the eve of his first step out of the city. He had carved it by moonlight, with Gods Whispers in his ears and prayers in his heart, and the Gods themselves had guided his hands. The divot in the top of the chest described a perfect hemisphere, and was filled at all times with water, and it was by the work of the Gods that not a drop ever spilled. Not when we climbed into the mountain passes; not when the earth itself shook beneath our feet. Never.

This was known to the people of the pilgrimage, and the story was never far from their minds. How could it be? They saw the chest every time we moved it from tent to wagon and back again, and the wood was worn smooth from the reverent touches they laid upon it whenever it was within reach. They knew that the tablets were inside the chest, and that it had been shaped by the shared intention of the Prophet and the Gods.

But they didn't know the final miracle of the chest. They didn't know that the water in the divot — the water which was freshened from my own waterskin every time that use and evaporation lowered the level to a shallow pool — landed salty on my tongue. Not the salt of my fingers, this; no. This was the thick, acid brine of the Gods' own tears.

The Prophet had explained it to me after I'd first prayed over the tablets. He'd said that the Gods were weeping for us, that they wept every time the sun rose and we were still not home in the Promised Land. He said that the taste of the saltwater was a reminder: the Gods are waiting.

As the bitterness faded from my tongue, the baby stirred in my belly. I pressed one hand to the chest that held the tablets, and said my prayer one more time before lifting the lid.

The tablets rested inside, wrapped in linen and pillowed on a bed of clean, dry timothy grass. They were ragged at the ends, broken pieces of massive bones, carved across the full breadth of their surfaces with trailing Gods Words. They were lighter than they looked.

I lifted the second tablet out, ignoring the first — the things predicted on that one had already come to pass.

"Please, O Gods," I whispered, "in your wisdom and mercy. Please tell me you have a plan to find us a new healer." Gods Whispers rustled as though from a great distance, and a shiver of worry hissed along the back of my neck.

I unwrapped the tablet and let my eyes fall to the etched bone.

To anyone without the Gods Sight — including me, until the night my father died — the markings looked like irregular, trailing scratches. But I could read them. By the grace of the Gods, through the Gods Sight gift my father had passed on to me before his death, I could read them.

I scanned the tablet over and over. I saw rain and loss and conflict and pain, but nothing about the loss of our healer. Nothing about how I was supposed to birth this baby without the help of a midwife.

"Please," I started to pray again, "please oh Gods, please, please—" but then there were gravel-crunching footsteps outside, running fast, and I barely had time to cover the tablet with linen before someone was bursting into my tent.

"Fisher— oh, Gods, I'm sorry." Rand, the child-minder, pulled up short, his sandals scuffing on the floor of my tent.

"It's fine, Rand," I said, carefully wrapping the tablet and placing it back into the chest. I closed the lid, slowly, reverently. I rose to my feet, wrapping my shawl more tightly around my shoulders to fight the chill of the rock flats, and faced him. "What is it?"

"We've lost one of the children," he said. His face was grey with fear. "We've looked everywhere, but she's gone. Mischa, Pinar's girl... she disappeared this morning while the children were playing look-and-find, and I can't—"

"Has a search party already been formed?" I asked briskly, already wrapping my feet in a few layers of wool. Rand wasn't wearing his — his feet were bare in his sandals, and his toes were white from the cold and the damp. I threw a roll of wrappings to him, and he wrapped his feet as he answered.

"Yes," he said, "and they're out in the flats now. I don't know if we'll find the girl, though, the fog is so thick—"

"We'll find her," I said. But I remembered the loss that was written on the tablets, and I wondered if this was what the Gods were warning me about.

"But, Prophetess," he said, his voice as soft as secrets. "I don't think she wandered off by accident, see?"

"What do you mean?" I whispered back, drawn in by the hush of his voice.

"I mean," he said, looking around as though there were ears inside my tent, "that I think maybe she was taken."

I laughed before I could stop myself, a short, sharp bark of surprise. "Taken? By who? Who would take a child?"

Rand was not amused, and his brow darkened. "Them you named last month, Fisher," he said grimly. "The outsiders. Everyone knows that Northerners have…" he paused significantly. "Appetites."

I threw an extra cloak over my shoulders, then made for the tentflap. Rand did not move out of my way, and I stared up at him with as much patience as I could muster. Rand was an ox of a man, perfect for child-minding, but he was stubborn, too.

"The outsiders," I repeated. "The outsiders, meaning, the woman and child we brought in?" He nodded. "The child being the one that you watch, the boy who's been helping feed the babies every day? And the woman being the one who taught your Magda how to bake a loaf without burning it? Those outsiders?"

Rand's jaw worked for a moment as he considered whether to dig in his heels. I could see him weighing his fear against his conscience.

Fear won.

"I don't trust them," he said. "They're not our people. I'm telling you, they're responsible for this."

I fastened my cloak and pushed past him. "Save your blame, Rand. There's no time now. I've got to talk to Pinar, and you've got to find Mischa. Go on."

At that moment, a wail rang out across the camp. I winced. It was unmistakably Pinar, Mischa's father. The news of his daughter's disappearance had reached him before I could. I bit back a curse and stepped out into the fog.

"Come on," I called back to Rand. "Let's find her."

CHAPTER SIX

Discovery

I HELD PINAR'S HAND as he wept for his daughter.

"I'm sorry," I said, and his shoulders shuddered. He was so thin — he hadn't eaten since Mischa went missing three weeks before. "I'm sorry," I said again. "We have to go."

He nodded. He knew that we were already risking everything by staying in the rock flats as long as we had — the grasslands waited, and the tablets were clear that we needed to reach them before the dead moon was in the sky if we were going to make it to the Promised Land at the appointed time. Still, he gripped me with the fervor of an argument.

"One more night," he whispered. "She'll come back. She has to."

"Pinar," I murmured. "We've sent out search parties as far as they can go. She's gone." I had practiced this part with Marc that morning, lying in our bed with his ear to my belly. "She's gone, and we have to leave."

"Leave me here, then," he said weakly. I leaned forward and pressed my lips to his forehead. My eyes were dry, and I clenched them shut.

"No," I said against his skin. When I walked out of his small tent, a hundred eyes were pretending not to watch me. I walked to the tent of the pathfinder to order the breaking of camp. Pinar's muffled sobs cut through the silent camp, and a hundred eyes looked away.

———

"Fisher." Jonah, my best scout, appeared through the fog just seconds after his footfalls announced him. "Prophetess, you have to come. You have to see— we found something."

"What is it?" I asked, and the boy looked up at me with shining eyes.

"Dinosaurs," he breathed.

We'd been driving the animals hard all day, and they were overdue for a rest anyway. I called a halt. The wagon train formed a rough circle, and Naomi took the sheep and goats out into the fog to find good grazing. I caught her arm as she passed.

"Don't go too far, all right?"

She nodded and gave my hand a squeeze. "You either," she said.

———

Jonah led me to the place where he'd found the dinosaurs. We rode mules, rude and short but nimble on the tricky parts of the rock flats where they transitioned into clay. The fog was thick and omnipresent, and I wondered how Jonah could possibly find his way — but then, that's why he was a scout.

"Look," he said.

I looked into the fog and saw nothing. "What?" I squinted.

"There." He tugged his mule's reins until it was right next to mine, and he pointed so that I could peer along his arm. There, perhaps four wagon-lengths in front of us, a shadow loomed out of the white.

"Oh," I said, and then I was off my mule and walking through sticky clay toward the shadow. "Oh," I said again.

He'd been telling the truth. Dinosaurs. Not live ones, of course — bones, huge skeletons half-buried, jutting out of the ground like a forest of branchless trees. I ran my hand along a massive, curved rib. As we walked into the field of bones, the fog thinned, and I could see entire skeletons — huge curving spines, and ribs that splayed out like spread fingers, their tips resting on the earth. Fins, their outlines still clear in the heavy soil, their bones like knuckles on the ground. Massive toothless skulls with long, strange mandibles. "The Prophet told me about dinosaurs he saw before I was born, but I never thought *I'd* see one," I whispered. "Gods be praised."

As soon as the blessing passed my lips, the Gods Whispers began, so loud I couldn't bear them. They were too much, too many, too fast and too sharp. I clapped my hands over my ears, but they only got louder. Animal panic made my heart stutter, and before I knew what I was doing I was running. I ran into the grove of bones, my feet slipping in the clay. I ran directly into the cathedral ribcage of one of the dinosaurs, finbones scattering behind me — and the Gods Whispers fell away.

The silence was overwhelming. I could hear my heartbeat thudding in my ears, the rasp of my breathing, Jonah's distant shouting. Overhead, arching ribs almost met. I looked down to see that I was standing on a half-buried vertebra: the creature had died on her back. I wiped at a tickle on my neck and my hand came away red: a trickle of blood was running from one of my ears.

"Gods," I wiped my hand on my cloak. The fog swirled in currents around me, and I laid a hand on the dinosaur's bone.

I snatched my hand back immediately, swearing, shaking my fingers — the bone had... *burned.*

"Fisher?" I ignored Jonah's distant shouts. I looked closer at the bone and saw that the place my blood had touched was steaming. Gods Whispers began again, soft this time, urgent.

As I watched, the Gods' own writing began to appear across the insides of the bones, spreading from the place that my blood had touched. I swallowed bile as the words appeared on each rib, glowing faintly red before darkening to black.

"Fisher, where are you?"

"I'll be right there," I called. I didn't move.

Betrayal. Salt. Deep. Cold. Good. Cold. Cold. Warmer. Warmer. Too warm, hot. Hot like fire. Far. Fear. Lost. Hot. Hungry. Hungry. Hungry. Hungry. Hungry.

That was it. I read the bones ten times over, and that was the message.

"What is this?" I murmured. "Is this even *for* me?"

"Fisher! Fisher, where are you! Fisher!" A note of urgency had entered Jonah's voice.

"Gods damn it," I muttered. I swore to myself that I would find my way back to the bones to read them again, to read them *right* this time.

"Coming," I shouted. I followed the sound of Jonah's voice until I found him. He was beside another dinosaur skeleton, this one half-buried on its side. Its ribs arced up out of the soil like a monstrous hand, and in the shelter of its fingers, Jonah hovered over a little lump on the ground.

"Fisher," Jonah said, "Fisher, it's her. I found her."

"What?"

"It's Mischa." He straightened, and the little lump in his arms resolved itself into a shape I almost recognized. Skeletal, unmoving, but unmistakable: Pinar's little girl.

The Gods Whispers rustled at me and I laid a hand on the girl's head. "She's alive?" I asked Jonah.

"I think so, but... not by much," he said.

"Gods preserve her," I prayed. I didn't stop praying until we had returned to the camp.

"Find Pinar," I said to the first ten people I saw. "Find him and tell him to come to my tent immediately."

By the time we arrived at my tent, a small crowd was trailing us. I held the tentflap open for Jonah, then turned to address the twenty people that stood in a semicircle around us.

"We need broth and..." I massaged my forehead. *I'm not a damn healer.* "Clove oil," I finally said. "And an extra brazier. Now, go, go!"

They scattered — all save for one figure. A boy. I didn't recognize him immediately, but after a moment the strange red highlights in his brown hair connected with a name.

"Samuel," I said. The foundling boy. I glanced over my shoulder at the entrance to my tent, then crouched in front of the child. "She'll be all right. You don't have to worry."

He wiped at his nose with one sleeve. "She's my best friend. I wanna see her."

I cursed myself for telling him that she would be all right: the girl had been wandering in the wilderness for weeks. She would almost certainly *not* be all right.

"I don't think that's a good idea," I said. The boy stared at me with those strange, mottled-green eyes, and then broke away at a run. He shoved me as he passed, sending me sprawling. I pushed myself to my feet, but he was already inside the tent.

"Samuel, no— *damn it*," I hissed, rubbing my raw palms on my thighs. Inside the tent, I heard Jonah echoing my exact words. Then, he cried out, louder and shrill.

"Samuel, what the— what are you *doing*, no, you can't—"

I ran into the tent, then pulled up short.

"Samuel," I said, speaking as softly as I could, "what are you doing?"

"I don't care if I get in trouble again," he answered. "She's my *friend*. And... it's my fault she's sick."

"What do you mean?"

"We were playing look-and-find and I told her that I bet she couldn't hide longest," he whispered, his face a mask of abject shame. "She hid so good that nobody could find her when it was time to break camp."

She hid, and then she couldn't find us, and she must have stumbled through the wilderness for weeks. It was a miracle she was still alive. I remembered the way that the dinosaur skeletons affected me — I wondered what impact they'd have on a child.

"It's my fault she's sick and I'm gonna help." Samuel's face was set into a stubborn knot of concentration. His hands hovered over Mischa, one over her face and one over her belly. Strands of black were flowing away from her, wrapping themselves around his wrists and arms and fingers like brambles. After a few seconds, he made a choked sound; then he ran outside, covered in black up to his elbows. As he ran, the black illness rose off his arms like mist. By the time he got to wherever he was running to, I knew, it would be as though it had never touched him.

In the bed, Mischa stirred.

"There's no way," Jonah said, looking up at me.

"Praise the Gods," I said, staring at the pink-cheeked, healthy little girl that lay in my bed. "It looks like they've sent us a new healer."

CHAPTER SEVEN

Storm

WHAT HAPPENED TO MARC WAS MY FAULT.

I was tired from a long night of counseling doubters and arbitrating quarrels, but that's not the point. On the dawn of the day the Prophet died, he told me that it was my fault. "Here's why you're nervous, Ducky," he had said, his voice thick and wet with the fluid that was collecting in his lungs. "You're nervous because from now on, everything that happens to these people is your fault. You're their prophet now. You're the one in charge of guiding them and protecting them."

He'd closed his eyes then and drawn a long, wincing breath. "You're right to be nervous," he'd said.

What happened to Marc was my fault.

I walked into our tent with my hands braced against my back. It felt like the baby was growing fast all of a sudden. It felt like everything that was happening was *all of a sudden*. Today, out of nowhere, an ache in my spine. What would it be tomorrow?

When I got into the tent, Marc was kneeling in front of the chest that held the sacred tablets. I didn't interrupt his prayer. I took off the dripping scarf that I'd had wrapped over my hair to keep the rain off, hung it near the brazier to dry.

I rubbed my hands together to warm them, listening to the thunder. After a few minutes, I settled onto our sleeping mat. Marc rose from his prayers and lay beside me, resting his palm on the crest of my belly.

"It's late," he said.

"Well, I had a lot to do," I snapped. I lifted his hand from my belly and kissed his palm in immediate apology, our usual way of acknowledging an unwarranted sharp word. He didn't kiss my knuckles in response. Instead, he pulled his hand back and frowned.

"You should be resting," he said, propping himself up on one elbow.

I laughed. "I'll rest in five months," I said.

His forehead creased. "But the baby is due in two months."

"...I'll rest when we reach the Promised Land," I said, staring at him. He didn't meet my eyes. "Marc," I said, and he shook his head, still not looking at me.

"Fisher," he said quietly. He returned his hand to my belly. I groaned, rubbing my hands across my face.

"No, Marc, no," I groaned. "I just spent *four hours* talking to people who don't think it's there. You can't—"

"Well, I'm sorry that it's hard to talk to your husband at the end of the day," he said petulantly. The baby pressed a foot to his palm. I rolled away so that he couldn't feel her reaching for him. It was petty, but it was satisfying.

"Marc, I can't do this with you," I said. "You're my husband. You are the *one* person here who is supposed to believe in me no matter what."

"I just think that we should have a backup plan," he said. "We're going to have a *baby*, Fisher—"

"I'm aware of that," I said. "I'm the one who's doing all the *work*—"

"What, I don't do enough? Is that what you're—"

"No," I said, my voice rising, "I just think that it's a little funny that *you're* telling *me* that we're having a baby when I'm the one who—"

"No, it's fine, I understand," he said, standing. "I hear you loud and clear, Fisher. I have to be the obedient, silent husband, right? While you're the big important Prophetess, I have to just—"

"Marc, come back to bed," I said, sitting up and massaging my temples. He reached for the tent flap, ignoring me. "Marc, don't go out there, the storm is crazy right now—"

"I can't be here with you right now," he said softly. "I can't have this fight with you."

"Marc," I called to him — but he was already outside. I heaved myself upright and ran to the tentflap, peeling it open to look out into the storm. The rain fell in sheets, ran in rivulets across the muddy gravel of the rock flats. He was stalking away from the tent, coatless, with his arms wrapped around his middle. "Marc," I called again. Thunder bellowed overhead, drowning me out. "Marc," I called one more time — but then, the lightning.

It was my fault.

The light was beyond blinding. For a blessed, Gods-gifted minute, I floated in a numb haze of silence and darkness, like sleep but panicked. I didn't realize that I was on my back until after the ringing in my ears faded. Then, my vision and my hearing returned, along with the ache in my spine, and I scrambled upright. "Marc!" I was screaming, and I raced outside. "Marc!"

He was flat on his back between my tent and Hanna's. His head was tipped back, smoking; his mouth gaped wide enough that I could see the dark shadow where he was missing a molar. Hanna, the Huntress, came outside at the sound of my screams.

"What happened to him?" she asked, running to where I was crouched next to my husband's lifeless, smoking body.

"Lightning," I said. "We have to get him inside before there's more, help, please help—" I was pulling on one of his arms, hot tears streaming down my cheeks. Hanna rested a hand on my wrist.

"There won't be more, Fisher," she said softly. "The rain's stopped."

I looked up. She was right — the clouds were already thinning, showing a few stars among the roiling mass of grey that was the sky.

"It'll be OK," she said, but her eyes said something different.

"Get the boy," I whispered.

"What?"

"Samuel," I said. "Get Samuel. Get the boy."

"Samuel? But why—"

"Just do it," I said. I crouched beside Marc, held his face in my hands, and prayed until footsteps slapped in the mud behind me. I whirled around to see the boy, Samuel, with his mottled-green eyes and strange, reddish hair. He was staring at Marc with wide, fearful eyes. I looked down at him, drawing myself up to my full height, trying to exude Prophetic authority. Hanna trailed behind the boy, watching me uncertainly.

"What happened to him?" Samuel asked.

"Lightning," I said. "He was struck by lightning, Samuel. I need you to heal him."

The boy started shaking his head, looking around as if someone would come and save him from this demand. "I can't—"

"You can," I said, "and you will." I stared at him with my black eyes, and he stared back into them with unmistakable terror. A tear spilled over his cheek.

"Please don't make me," he said. "My mother will—" I grabbed his little shaking hands in mine, and he fell silent. He tried to pull away, but I gripped his fingers tight.

"Save him."

———

Maia burst into my tent, breathless. "Where's my son?" she said, the fervent fury of a mother in her voice.

"I'm here, Mama," he said, rising from his place beside the sleeping mat. His arms were covered in a thick coat of foul, sparking white.

"Oh, baby, no," she whispered. "What have you done?"

"I helped him," Samuel said, his eyes on the floor. Maia slapped him as fast and hard as the lightning strike that had flattened Marc.

"You know you can't," she hissed, gripping Samuel's shoulder and shaking it. "You know you *can't*, they'll — don't you remember that happened last time?" Samuel choked on a sob, and Maia turned to me with stark fear. "Please," she said, "he won't do it again, please don't punish him—"

I shook my head, held my hands out to her without touching her. "No," I said, "You don't understand — I told him to do it. I made him."

She blinked at me. "How did you — did he tell you that he could do this?"

"No," I said quickly, "no, he did it once before — he saved Mischa's life when we found her last month. I was going to wait until he was older and then find someone to train him as a healer, but tonight..."

All of the air went out of her. "So you're not going to make us leave?"

I rested a hand on her shoulder, gentle as I could manage, and spoke softly. "Why would we make you leave?"

"Because of Samuel's curse," she said, her voice breaking as a shiver passed through her.

From behind her, a low voice rasped. "No. Not a curse."

We all looked to Marc. Blood vessels in his eyes had burst, staining the whites red. "Not a curse," he said again. "Never a curse." He reached for Samuel, rested a hand on the boy's calf. "The Gods give only gifts, Samuel. You are beloved of the Gods, and they have given you a great gift. Pray your thanks."

I fell to my knees. I touched Marc's face, his throat, his chest. I whispered his name, had no idea how to say what needed saying.

"Fisher," he said, grasping one of my hands. Behind me, Maia was murmuring to Samuel, something low and firm. I knew I'd need to talk to both of them later, to plan how to develop the boy's gift, but for now, there was only Marc, alive. *Alive.* "Prophetess," he said. He coughed, and I tried not to weep.

"Marc, I'm sorry—"

He shook his head. "I saw them, Prophetess."

I blinked at him. "What?"

"I saw them," he said. "I saw the Promised Land. I saw the Gods. It's real, it's all real."

"You — what?" I said. "You saw the Promised Land?"

"Help me up," he said. "I have to pray. I have to pray thanks. It was beautiful, Fisher. They're — they're amazing. Like clouds, like plums, like moons... like nothing you've ever seen. I have to pray thanks. Help." He started trying to struggle upright. I rested a hand on his chest, pushed him down.

"Pray later," I said. "Marc, you were struck by lightning. You need rest. You almost died."

He shook his head. "The Gods send only gifts," he murmured. "The Gods send only gifts."

CHAPTER EIGHT

Anticipation

MY BONES ACHED AND SPREAD as we crossed into the grassy flatlands, but I did not stop walking. I set my feet into the red-brown half-moon footprints that Naomi left on the earth in front of me, feeling almost at home in the soft sadness of missing my own monthly blood.

I would wonder later if that nostalgia is what brought on my own blood.

It wasn't much — not enough to add to Naomi's footprints. But it was enough to make me summon the healer-foundling once we stopped to rest.

"Sam, come here," I said. The boy ran to me, his legs swinging coltishly underneath him. He was the human embodiment of a growth spurt, all awkward elbows and skinny ankles.

"Yes, Fisher?" He ducked his head and I frowned.

"Why are you doing that?"

"What?"

"Bowing," I said. "People have been doing that lately, when they talk to me. Why? None of you ever bowed to me before."

Sam rubbed the back of his neck. "Well, I don't know," he mumbled. "I guess... ever since Marc got struck by lightning, he's been going around telling everyone that it's all real."

I felt my frown deepen. "So?"

"So..." he shrugged. "So I guess it seems more real now."

"It doesn't matter," I muttered to myself.

"What?" Sam asked. I shook my head.

"Nothing. Sam, I need you to check on the baby. Go get Naomi so she can help tell you what you're looking at."

Ever the pliant boy, Sam raced off to find Naomi, my best friend and the woman in charge of our livestock. While he was gone, I breathed deeply and reminded myself that it didn't matter why people were believing. All that mattered was that they *believed*. So what if the only thing that made them follow their Prophetess was the testimony of her newly pious husband? I prayed my thanks, although the Gods surely tasted the bitterness in my heart. I was still praying when Sam and Naomi returned.

"Are you all right?" Naomi asked in the same low voice I'd heard her use to calm anxious goats.

"I'm sure I'm fine," I said, trying to sound calm. "It's just... I started bleeding around midday, and it hasn't stopped yet."

"But she's not supposed to bleed until after the baby comes," Sam said, looking to Naomi for verification. Naomi nodded to him, and I looked between the two, wondering what lessons the boy had been learning from her.

"Let's take a look," Naomi said. She nodded to Sam, and he rested his palms on my belly. After a moment, I felt the questing, flickering warmth of his gift.

"Is it the same as with the goats?" Sam asked.

Naomi shook her head. "Not quite. Just tell me what you see and we'll figure it out together, OK?"

Sam nodded slowly, then looked to Naomi with some alarm. "The baby is underwater," he whispered.

"That's good," she said. "Those are the waters of the womb, remember?"

He didn't answer, frowning. He described everything that he saw and felt. The speed of the baby's heartbeat, which made Naomi frown. The quiet warmth of my womb, the softening of my joints. The push and pull of my pulse.

After nearly an hour of this, Naomi shook her head. "I don't know," she whispered.

"What don't you know?" I asked. She closed her eyes.

"I don't know what's wrong. Maybe a tear in the placenta? I'm not sure."

I looked to Sam. "Can you fix it?"

He lifted his shoulders. "I don't know how," he said.

Naomi twisted a lock of her short, curly hair between two fingers, an old, anxious habit that always grated on my nerves. "How do you feel?"

"Like a dinosaur," I snapped. "Like a monstrously huge beast that can't *rest* because everything is too *hot* and—" I cut myself off. *Shit.* I'd promised myself I wouldn't talk about the dinosaur boneyard I'd found, the Gods Words etched into the ribs of one of the great beasts.

"Um..." Naomi was looking at me as though I'd grown an extra leg out of my forehead. "What?"

"Nevermind," I said quickly. "Nevermind, I just... I'm tired, is all."

She stood, dusting off her palms. "Well, you won't be tired for long," she said. "We're staying here. I'll tell the group that you need to—"

"Wait," I said, grabbing her leg. "No. Tell them..." I glanced at Sam, who was watching me with rapt attention. "Tell them one of the oxen pulled up lame," I said, lowering my voice as though that would keep the boy from hearing his Prophetess tell a lie.

Naomi nodded. "Fine," she said. "But that will only buy us a few days."

"I'll figure something out," I snapped. Naomi left, taking Sam with her.

I rested a palm on the swell of my belly and wondered what unasked-for gift the Gods were trying to give me this time.

—

I must have fallen asleep in the middle of my prayers. When I opened my eyes, it was dark; my hand still rested over the shifting hill of my baby. Outside of my tent, voices rose and fell like waves crashing on some distant shore.

I struggled to sit up, listened to the voices outside. There was a rumble of wheels, a shout, a thump. By the time I made it to the tentflap and looked outside, the commotion had passed. Sam sat outside of my tent, a fresh bruise swelling under one eye.

"Sam?" I asked. "What's going on, what happened? Who hit you?"

He raised his fingers to his eye. "They're leaving," he said. He looked up at me, tears shining in his eyes.

"Who's leaving? Where's Naomi?"

Naomi ran up to me, breathless, Marc trailing behind her. "I'm sorry, Fisher," she said. "I couldn't stop them."

"What happened?" I said. I didn't realize I'd shouted until I looked at their shocked faces.

"Hanna, Liam, Rand... a few others," she said. "They're leaving. They took the seed and water wagons. They said they'll meet us at the Promised Land."

"But— no," I said, "no, they can't— what?" I felt like I'd swallowed a live bird, like it was frantically beating at the inside of my throat and chest, trying to escape.

"They checked the oxen," Sam muttered. "They looked and saw that none of them were lame and they said that—"

"Don't, Sam," Marc warned. Sam shut his mouth and stared at the ground, sullen.

"But that's all of our seeds, all of our water, all of the feed for the animals—" my head swam.

"The animals will eat grass, and we'll find a stream, I'm sure," Naomi said. "We're so close, Fisher. We'll make it."

I pressed at my temples with the heels of my hands. "We have to," I whispered. "Just five more months and we'll be at the Promised Land. The tablets said—"

"The Gods said," Marc corrected me. "The Gods are leading us to them. Even if there's no water anywhere between here and the Promised Land, we'll make it there." He rested a hand on my shoulder and I leaned into the warmth of his palm.

"Prophetess," Sam said. I looked up, followed his gaze.

Four dark drops of blood had fallen to the dust between my feet.

"We'll make it," Marc said again, his eyes on the sharp crescent of the moon overhead. "Sooner than we know."

CHAPTER NINE

Sundering

THE TABLETS FORETOLD THE SHADOW that passed over the moon on the day of my daughter's birth.

The pain was worse than I had feared and better than I had hoped. It was consuming and distant, a fire at my feet and water in my lungs. It was everything, and then my daughter cried for the first time, and the pain was nothing at all.

The tablets foretold the shadow, but they did not tell me how I would reach down between my legs and feel my daughter's head there. They did not tell me how soft her hair would already be, before she even finished emerging into the world. She had dark hair. Like mine.

I held her to my chest and I whispered into that dark hair, which smelled of musk and blood. "I name you Ducky, daughter of Fisher." She kept breathing on my chest, her ribs flexing with every breath. Her eyes were shut tight. I ran a fingertip across the soft, narrow curl of her ear.

Naomi came crashing through the tall grasses a moment later.

"Fisher?" she looked frantic. She saw me, lying there on a bed of bent stalks with blood pooling around me. "Fisher, oh my Gods, Fisher where have you—" And then she saw the baby. "Fisher, wh— what is, what is that?" She stammered, ran a hand through her own blonde curls. "What did you—are you— is she—"

"We're both fine," I murmured into Ducky's hair. "We were born tonight, weren't we, Ducky?"

The shadow passed away from the moon, and my daughter opened her eyes to look blearily up at the sudden light

—

It was a Godsmoon that night, as full and lush and round as I felt. The tablets foretold the shadow. They hadn't said how long it would linger. I had never seen a shadow pass over the moon before. Most of us stayed inside on the nights that the shadow was due — it was an awful thing, a dark thing. It was a silencing of the Gods' own brightness. When the tablets predicted a shadow over a Godsmoon, it was a warning: let there be no feasts on this night, no celebrations, no dancing. Go to bed early and stay there until daylight.

But on his deathbed, the Prophet had told me about the shadow. He had told me about the first time he had defied the Gods.

"It was just after your mother died," he'd said. "You had a fever, and the Gods Whispers were relentless, telling me that danger was on the way, and greater loss than I'd ever known." The Gods Whispers had been right — I remembered that season of torment. My mother and ten others had died of the fever, and then, not a month later, a whole wagon of seed had fallen off a cliffside, taking three children with it. "They wouldn't stop, wouldn't quiet, and I was going out of my mind, Ducky, you have to understand." I had tried to offer him a cup of water, but he waved it away. "I went outside, just to get some air. I'd forgotten that the shadow was coming, and when I walked outside, it was passing over the Godsmoon."

"You saw it?" I'd gasped.

"I saw it, and as it crossed over the Godsmoon, Ducky... the Gods were quiet."

I'd been horrified at him. He was telling me that he had voluntarily silenced the voices of the Gods. "How could you?" I'd whispered.

"Oh, Ducky," he'd said, patting my hand. He closed his eyes, remembering. "After that, I went outside every time the shadow passed over the Godsmoon. You'll understand."

"I'll never understand that," I'd snapped. "I would never silence the Gods."

But then, my belly was ripe to bursting and a quarter of my people fled from me to find the Promised Land for themselves, and the Gods Whispers were constant and urgent, insisting that there was always more to do, that my work wasn't done yet and never would be. And then there were waves of pain, and the Gods Whispers had grown louder with every single one.

And I found that I did understand, after all.

———

Later, after Ducky and I were both clean and dry and warm, Marc asked me why I did it. "Why didn't you tell me where you were going?" he asked.

"I didn't know," I said. It was mostly a lie. I had slipped out of our bed in the night to relieve myself for the third time — or the fourth, I couldn't be sure — and the baby came while I was outside. That's what I told him, and Naomi, and anyone who asked. But the truth is that I had known she was on the way. My waters had broken that morning, and the pain had been building throughout the day.

When I left my tent that night and walked out into the tall grasses of the plain, I knew that I would be coming back with a baby in my arms.

Naomi was furious, of course. She should have been there, and Marc, and Sam, just in case I needed a healer. Just in case the baby needed a healer. But the tall grasses beckoned, and I wanted to watch the shadow pass over the moon.

And maybe I wanted to be alone. Just for a moment. Maybe I wanted to be a woman birthing her first child, and not the voice of the Gods to their fearful, exhausted, thirsty people. Maybe I wanted a moment of silence, a moment to be alone with the pain and the fear and my own animal need to scream.

"I didn't know that she would come so fast," I told Marc when he asked why I did it. And that was true — I didn't know how suddenly she would slide out of me, how hard it would be to catch her before she touched the ground.

But I knew she was coming. How could I not know? She was mine.

CHAPTER TEN

Nearness

DUCKY HAD JUST FINALLY FALLEN ASLEEP when the rear flap of canvas on the back of my wagon snapped open.

"You need to see this."

I nearly screamed with frustration as Ducky's head jerked. Her eyes fluttered open, and she drew breath to start wailing. Again.

"What is it, Marc?" I snapped. The tablets say not to hate anyone, and so I did not hate my husband. But I was not particularly in love with him that day, either. He'd taken to praying through the night, refusing to interrupt his devotion to the Gods even when Ducky stirred and cried. Even when I hadn't slept for days.

"You need to come, Prophetess," he said, inclining his head in the formal bow that most of my followers had taken to performing. I wanted to throw something at him.

"Fine," I said through gritted teeth. I climbed from the moving wagon, stumbling as I landed. It was loud outside of the wagon — the noise of the wheels crunching through the gravelly dirt of the scrubland combined with the shouts of the children who ran behind us, waving sticks and occasionally hitting each other. The wagons were moving at a fervent pace. Marc tried to get me to follow him, but I ignored him, planting my feet until Naomi caught up to us.

"Can you take Ducky?" I asked, handing my daughter to her before she could answer. "Apparently I'm needed."

"Oh, I'll say," she replied, her ruddy face grim. "I already had Sam pull a mule for you. Hino is waiting for you up front."

"Hino? Jasper's boy?"

"He took over as lead scout when Jonah... um." She trailed off, and I didn't answer. I started off toward the front of the wagon train, half-jogging to beat the pace we were setting. I lifted my hand in thanks without looking back.

What she hadn't said — what she hadn't been willing to remind me — was that Jonah had left along with nineteen other Children of the Gods. Back between Marc's awakening and Ducky's birth, I'd lost twenty followers, along with all the stored water and the seed that we'd been able to save throughout all of the floods and storms and fires and deserts we'd survived.

Everyone who remained had been wonderful during the long month of my confinement, labor, and recovery. But now we were behind schedule, and we needed to catch up to the brothers and sisters who had abandoned us. They'd sworn to follow the trail mapped out by the Gods. They'd sworn to meet us in the Promised Land.

So after Ducky's birth, we jettisoned every scrap of weight that we could spare, and we raced to meet them.

"This way, Prophetess," the boy who met me at the front of the wagon train said. He waved an arm at me as I mounted the mule that was waiting.

"Hino, right?" I asked as we began to ride ahead of the group. "When did you get so tall?"

"I'm not sure, Prophetess," he said. I shifted uncomfortably on the mule's back.

"Where are we going?"

He didn't answer, and I watched his face as he stopped himself from — what? Crying? Vomiting? We rode in silence for the time it took sweat to begin etching a course through the grit on my back. Hino stopped next to a broad swath of scrub, and helped me off my mule.

"Hino, what's here?" The sun seemed to be perched directly on top of us. The bleached-blue expanse of the sky was broken only by a few huge black birds, circling in the distance. I wiped at my face with one corner of the scarf I wore whenever we crossed through sands or scrubland.

"Come with me, please," he replied, and his eyes begged me not to make him explain. I reminded myself that Marc and Naomi had both thought I should come with this young man, and I swallowed back my doubts.

We picked our way through the scrub, leading our mules, dodging spiny leaves that attempted to gouge our legs. Sweat stung my eyes, and I wished that I'd worn a less threadbare scarf over my dark hair to keep the sun from cooking my scalp. My eyes were on the ground, and I nearly bumped into Hino when he stopped short in front of me.

"There," he said, pointing. It took a moment for my eyes to follow his finger. At first I thought he was pointing to the shadow of the great bird that circled overhead.

Then, the shadow passed, and I saw them. They were lined up like pearls on a necklace: twenty heads, arranged from largest to smallest. They looked strange, gape-mouthed and staring, and it took me a moment to realize that their eyes, lips, and tongues had been removed.

"What... what happened to them?" I asked, hearing how stupid I sounded even as the words left my mouth.

"Scavengers, most like," Hino answered. "They always go for the softest parts first."

"What came before the scavengers?" I wondered aloud.

I moved closer and crouched in front of the heads, staring into the faces. Even mutilated as they were, I recognized them. On one end, the massive head of Rand, the child-minder. On the opposite end, the tiny head his daughter. I paced along the line, looking into each of their faces.

Jonah, the old scout, was somewhere in the middle.

"Who did this to you?" I whispered. The Gods replied with only the faintest of murmurs. I closed my eyes, trying to listen harder.

The Gods whispered "justice" in my ear.

"No," I muttered. "No, this is not justice. This is not right."

The Gods had no answer for that.

"Where are their bodies?" I asked Hino. He shrugged, studying a tick on his mule's back. "Who killed them? Why?" He shrugged again, although I hadn't expected an answer to those questions.

I scrubbed my face with both hands, trying to discern what message I was meant to take from this display.

"I, um, I found the wagons, Prophetess." He cleared his throat. "They're just over that ridge."

Hope swelled in me like a rising tide.

"They're burned out," he said. "Seeds and all. Unsalvageable." He wouldn't look at me.

I breathed heavily through my nose. "Shit," I spat. "Shit."

"Prophetess?" Hino said softly. I looked back and saw that he was still staring at his mule's back. He wiped at his face with the back of one arm.

"What is it, Hino?"

"Would... would you pray with me?" He looked up at me, and his face was as broken as a dropped egg.

The Gods' own stillness settled over me like a mantle. I walked over to him, rested my hand on his shoulder. "Of course, my son," I said, my voice heavy with comfort and authority. The buzzard that had been circling overhead landed heavily behind me, having finally decided that I wasn't a threat. As it began tearing the flesh off one of the faces that rested in the line on the ground, I prayed to the Gods for mercy, comfort, and peace. Under my hand, Hino's shoulders shuddered.

In the distance, I heard the oncoming rumble of our wagon train, catching up to us at last.

CHAPTER ELEVEN

Recognition

I STARED AT THE CHEST THAT CONTAINED THE TABLETS. I couldn't tear
my eyes away from the water that rested in the divot on top
of the chest. The sacred water — the Gods tears, shed for
their sadness in missing their children. The divot was carved
into the wood, deep and narrow. Salt crystals filmed the
edges of the divot, white and patchy, interrupted only by a
single dark smear of blood.

I stared at the blood, trying to make sense of what I was
seeing. It was old blood, brown and flaking, but I knew that
it was blood the same way that I would have known my own
daughter's cry from the cries of a hundred other children.

My memory darted between the present moment and
a moment three weeks before, the night before I found
the dismembered heads of the dissenters that had left our
camp to find the Promised Land for themselves. It had been
the middle of the night, and Ducky had been stirring and
grumbling, and I had woken to take care of her.

Marc had been kneeling beside the chest.

He was praying, and I remembered stifling bitter
resentment at the sight of him on his knees, attempting
to commune with the Gods while I cared for our child. I
remembered watching him touch his fingers to the top of the

chest, and I remembered thinking that I should tell him not to. That I should tell him the water in the divot was intended only for the Prophetess of the Gods.

In the aftermath of finding those twenty half-eaten heads in the desert, I had forgotten to tell him. It was important, but I was taking care of my people and I forgot to tell him. But I thought back now, as I stared at that drop of blood, and I tried to remember if Marc had been wearing his sandals or not. I tried to remember if there had been a pink tint to the wash water in our basin the next morning. I tried to remember if I'd seen him wearing those same clothes again, or if they'd disappeared.

The more I tried to remember, the larger the blood loomed before me. The more I tried to remember, the louder the Gods whispered: *Look, Fisher. Look at what he has done*.

———

That night, I pretended to sleep until Marc eased himself onto the sleeping mat beside me. I startled awake, grabbed at him, pushed my face into the crook of his shoulder and allowed myself the shudder I'd been suppressing all day.

"Oh," he said softly, his arm rising to wrap around me. "What is it, love? Are you all right?"

His hands were so gentle. His breath stirred the hair on top of my head, and I remembered that I loved him. *Look at what he has done*. "I had a nightmare," I said, and the tremor in my voice was real.

"It wasn't real," he murmured, pressing his lips to the top of my head. "It wasn't real, you're safe. It's all right."

I swallowed hard, forced myself to continue. "It was awful," I whispered. "It was like I was back there all over again, in the desert."

Marc didn't say anything for long enough that I feared he'd fallen asleep. Beside our bed, the baby shifted. Finally, Marc spoke. "The dissenters?"

"Yes," I said, too loudly. Ducky made a low noise in her sleep, and I reminded myself to whisper. "Yes," I repeated, "the dissenters — it was so horrible, Marc, their faces... some of them were *children*, and I—"

"I'm sure it was hard to see," Marc replied. He began to rub my back in small circles. "Sometimes the Gods' justice is difficult to take in."

"Justice?" I asked. Marc was very still beside me.

"Yes," he said. "It must have been awful for you, having to see that. But surely you agree that it's no less than what they deserved?"

I pulled away from him, stared at him hard even though he was just a vague patch of darkness in the shadows of our tent. "No," I said, forgetting my volume again. "No one deserves that. They didn't—"

"They strayed from the Gods' path," Marc said, also too loud, and his voice was a cliff's edge. "Whoever killed them did them a favor. They were spared a life of sin."

Ducky began to cry. I reached for her without needing to see where she was. Her forehead was hot against my shoulder, and I patted her back, blowing on her neck to cool her off. "Who would do such a thing?" I asked Marc. "Who would slaughter those children? They were innocents, Marc."

"Innocents who stole seeds and water from the Children of the Gods," he said. He was breathing hard, and I could hear him twisting the blanket between his fists. "Innocents who abandoned their people."

I shook my head. Ducky had fallen back asleep moments after I'd picked her up, but I didn't want to put her down. Not yet. I couldn't find words. Marc reached up a hand and tugged gently on my shoulder, pulling me back down to lie beside him. "Hush, Prophetess," he murmured, his lips against my temple again. "It was only a bad dream. The Gods will never let any harm befall those who follow their path."

Ducky rested on my chest, her belly rising and falling with each deep breath she took. Marc's hand found her, and he stroked her hair. "Who would do such a thing?" I whispered again.

"Shhh. Go to sleep," he whispered. "There's nothing to fear."

The Gods Whispers nearly drowned him out. *Look*, they said to me. *Look at what you have done.*

CHAPTER TWELVE

Arrival

I STOOD AT THE CLIFF'S EDGE and stared at the tablet in my hands as the first stars of the evening appeared in the bruise-black sky.

Here, here, here, here, here. The words swam across the etched bone and echoed in my bones.

"This is it," I called to the gathered crowd behind me. "We're here."

Here, here, here, here.

"This can't be it," a voice cried back.

"It's impossible," said another.

"Shut up," said a third, and I recognized it as Samuel, the healer-boy.

Here.

"Look — in the water." Samuel again. "What is that?"

———

Everyone had been in a festival mood for the preceding week. Every last one of the Children of the Gods knew the timeline of the tablets backwards and forwards. *On the first night of the dead moon in the Thirty-First year, the Children of the Gods shall cross out of the scrubland and into the Promised Land. Rich hunting and plentiful fish and good, clear waters await you, and your spawn shall be many, and no harm shall befall you from above or below.* The Gods had never lied to us. We had weathered flood and famine and fire and fever, all with their guidance. We had wandered through the desert, the rock flats, the grassland, the mountains — we had seen loss and endured fear, and the Gods had always told us that we would make it through.

Everyone, even my most troubled followers, had been looking to the horizon all week. They would trail off in the middle of sentences, staring into the distance, their eyes bright. *It's there*, they would whisper to each other. *Just over that hill, just around the corner. The Promised Land. It's there.*

———

Marc ran up, Ducky clutched in his arms. She was fighting at her swaddling clothes, and as Marc pulled up short beside me, Ducky wrenched an arm free. She grabbed at a lock of my hair as it flailed in the cold wind that blew off the sea in front of us.

"Is this it?" Marc asked, his eyes fever-bright. He grinned so widely that I could see the shadow of his missing molar.

"I... it can't be," I said, searching his face for a sign of doubt. There was none — his faith was as intense and un-wavering as the lightning that had instilled it in him. "This can't be the Promised Land, Marc. There's no land here." I was ashamed at the note of pleading in my voice. "It's all scrubland behind us, there's no — this isn't — stone and sea don't make land."

"It is, though, Fisher. It's their land. Don't you see?" He peered over the cliff's edge. His sandal sent pebbles skittering down the cliffside; they landed in the water below, close enough that I could hear the splash but too far for me to see the ripples. A vast moon shone in the water. "They're inviting us. We can join them. All we have to do is trust."

I blinked. I looked up at the sky and rubbed my eyes with the hand that did not hold the Gods' tablet. "This can't be, Marc. Maybe... maybe they just don't understand?" I let out a hoarse laugh. "We can't live underwater. This can't be it."

There was no moon in the sky. It was a dead moon — the great bowl of the God's light was empty.

But there it was, floating in the water below us.

Cries rose up behind me as my followers began to notice the light. I held up a hand to silence them, and listened hard for the Gods Whispers to tell me what to do.

Here, they repeated, maddeningly persistent, *here, here, here, here, here*.

In the water, another moon rose. And another, and another — and then there were dozens of them, hundreds, green-white and bobbing gently with the rocking of the sea. Tendrils floated between some of them, drifting with the motion of the water. *Here, here, here, here, here.*

"Do you hear them?" Marc asked, absentmindedly patting Ducky's back with one hand. "Do you hear them, Fisher?"

I snapped my eyes to him. "What?"

"The Gods," he said. A smile had spread across his face; his eyes were locked on the water.

"What do you hear?" I asked him.

He looked up at me and pointed to the water. "The Gods," he said again. "They're here."

I would wonder later if I had reached for him or for Ducky. I would wonder if I had seen something in his face, illuminated by the bright light from below. Had I tried to save them both, or had I hoped to catch only one?

It didn't matter, either way. My hands closed around a corner of swaddling cloth, and a too-small weight fell into my arms, and Ducky began to scream against my shoulder as Marc plummeted silently to the water below.

———

We made our way down the cliffside single-file, the pack animals left behind. I stumbled across the rocky slope in front of everyone, my hands and face numb with the stinging, frigid wind that whipped up off the water. I clutched the baby to my chest with one arm. I couldn't hear anything over the wind and Ducky's ceaseless crying, but my way was lit by the glow that still came off the water. There was a narrow strip of rocky shore between the cliff and the water, and when my feet met the ground, they ached with cold.

I turned to face the water, and the wind stilled. Gentle waves lapped at the shore, dampening my feet.

The moons parted. As I watched, a shadow passed through them. Each wave brought it closer, pushing it toward me and then pulling it back. I did not move. Behind me, the Children of the Gods packed themselves onto the tiny beach, watching me watch the ocean.

"What is it?" someone whispered.

"Hush," came the sharp reply.

I stepped into the water, shaking with fear and cold. As the water rose past my knees, the waves stilled. One of the moons in the water reached out a long tendril and wrapped it around my calf. It looked like a loving gesture, but it hurt. Oh, Gods, it hurt. It was everything I could do not to drop Ducky, everything I could do not to faint. The pain was a stripe of bright fire — but then the tendril withdrew, and when I looked into the water to see whether my blood was pinking the brine, the shadow was there, bumping against my shins.

I held the Gods' tablet out to Samuel. "Take this," I said, and he hesitated until I turned to glare at him. He took the tablet with the same tender reverence I'd seen on Marc's face the first time he'd held Ducky.

I pushed the thought away. I held Ducky a little tighter as I bent over the water. With my free hand, I reached into the freezing sea, soaking my tunic to the elbow, and grabbed it.

It was hard. Small — just large enough to be tricky to grab with just one hand. I scooped my palm underneath it and lifted it out of the sea. I held it up, and the light that shone from the water illuminated it in my hands.

It was a skull. The jawbone was gone. A tuft of blonde hair clung to the crown of it. Blood streaked the insides of the eye sockets, the places between the teeth. It smelled of salt and iron.

One of the molars was missing.

"Marc," I whispered. "No."

The moons in the water came closer, nearly touching me. Ducky turned her head toward the light, reaching with one arm toward the water. In their glow, I saw that Gods Words scarred the skull, burned blood darkening the streaks of lettering. The words swam before my eyes, just as they did on the sacred tablets. They resolved themselves into a message:

Who are you who cannot come home to us? You are not the ones we sent for.

fin

Sarah Gailey

HUGO AND CAMPBELL AWARD FINALIST SARAH GAILEY lives and works in beautiful Oakland, California. Her nonfiction has been published by *Mashable* and *The Boston Globe*, and her fiction has been published internationally. She is a regular contributor for Tor.com and Barnes & Noble. You can find links to her work at ***sarahgailey.com***.
She tweets ***@gaileyfrey***.

CONTENT NOTE

for

The Fisher of Bones

..

Chapter Ten: Nearness contains
one scene of moderate intensity
concerning child death.

Fireside Fiction Company provides content notes for its books
to guide readers who may wish to seek out or avoid particular story
elements. A current list of all the elements covered in our content
notes can be found at ***firesidefiction.com/about/#content-notes***. We
welcome your suggestions for elements to include or exclude.

Legend:
- •   One scene of mild intensity
- ••   One scene of moderate intensity
- •••   Multiple scenes of mild to moderate intensity
- ••••   One scene of high intensity
- •••••   Multiple scenes of high intensity

A Note to our Readers

Thank you so much for reading *The Fisher of Bones*. We hope you enjoyed it! If you did, we encourage you to leave a review somewhere like Amazon or Goodreads. Reviews are really vital to helping spread the word about our books.

If you like what we do and want to help us do more of it, check out ***firesidefiction.com*** and become one of our backers.

The body text in *The Fisher of Bones* is set in Cordale, from the Dalton Maag foundry, and the headlines are set in Zalamander, from Just Another Foundry.

Made in the USA
Middletown, DE
21 February 2019